I0803911

POLICE OFFICERS
ON THE SCENE

BY EMILY DOLBEAR

The Child's World®
childsworld.com

Published by The Child's World®
1980 Lookout Drive • Mankato, MN 56003-1705
800-599-READ • www.childsworld.com

Photographs: John Roman Images/Shutterstock.com, cover, 1; Harry Hu/Shutterstock.com, 5; Alex Segre/Shutterstock.com, 6; Scott Terrell/*The Skagit Valley Herald* via AP, 8; Photo Spirit/Shutterstock.com, 10; US Army/Yvonne Najera, 13; Julian Leshay/Shutterstock.com, 14; Jelani Photography/Shutterstock.com, 17; Uwe Lubjuhn/Shutterstock.com, 18; bibiphoto/Shutterstock.com, 20

Copyright © 2022 by The Child's World®
All rights reserved. No part of this book may be reproduced or utilized in any form or by any means without written permission from the publisher.

ISBN 9781503855823 (Reinforced Library Binding)
ISBN 9781503856158 (Portable Document Format)
ISBN 9781503856394 (Online Multi-user eBook)
LCCN: 2021940167

Printed in the United States of America

TABLE OF CONTENTS

FAST FACTS

What's the Job?

- Police officers protect people and property. They are responsible for enforcing laws and maintaining community safety. They also prevent and investigate crimes.
- Many police officers have graduated from college. They all attend police academy. Then they complete on-the-job training.
- Police officers must pass physical and written tests. Some skills, such as knowledge of a second language, are also helpful. Officers do not have a criminal record, which means they have not been arrested in the past for committing a crime.
- Most police officers work for their local or state government. Others work for federal law enforcement agencies.

The Dangers

- Police work can be physically demanding. The job can also be stressful and dangerous.
- Police officers sometimes die in the line of duty. In the United States, 135 police officers died at work in 2019. The deaths were a result of criminal acts or car accidents. In 2020, there were 264 on-the-job deaths. At least 145 were due to **COVID-19**.

Important Stats

- There are about 800,000 police officers and detectives in the United States.
- Police officers earn about $67,000 a year.
- Through 2029, the need for police officers will likely grow faster than average.

PINA COL
CROS
SEIDITA

Chapter 1

ON PATROL DUTY

A call from the **dispatcher** crackled over their police radio. Someone had heard panicked screams and called 911. A child was unresponsive. The address was on Third Avenue East in Newark, New Jersey.

Luckily, the two patrol officers were just a block away. A quick turn in their black-and-white cruiser brought them to the red brick house. There had not even been time to turn on their lights or siren. The officers leaped out of the car, leaving the doors open. Only 90 seconds had passed.

It was a hot July afternoon. Officers Shaquille Jackson and Malikul Aziz were baking in their dark uniforms. Each wore a bulletproof vest under his short-sleeved shirt. Around their waists were heavy police **duty belts**. Each belt held a radio, handcuffs, a flashlight, and a firearm.

◀ Police officers patrol the streets. An officer's main duty is enforcing laws and keeping the community safe.

▲ **911 dispatchers send police officers to all kinds of emergencies, including medical emergencies. Police officers have first aid training and can give basic medical care.**

The officers had been on the job for less than a year. As **rookies**, they still had many things to learn. And every call was captured on **body camera** video.

In the front yard, plastic toys floated in a standing pool. A two-year-old wearing a wet bathing suit was in distress. She was not breathing.

Shaquille quickly turned the limp victim over in his hands. He hit her firmly between the shoulder blades. Again and again, the officer thumped the child's back. He tried to force the water from her lungs as he had been trained. Malikul helped hold the small, slippery body.

For several tense moments, the victim made no noise. The neighbor who had called 911 stood by anxiously. Then, finally, the little girl coughed and began to cry. The adult who had been watching her breathed a sigh of great relief.

It turned out the toddler had flipped over in the pool while swimming. Wearing two inflatable rings, she had struggled under the water. It's dangerous to take your eyes off kids in the water, Shaquille warned, even for a minute. By then, an ambulance had arrived. The paramedics examined the little girl and monitored her vital signs. Vital signs are a person's heart rate, breathing rate, temperature, and blood pressure.

The rest of the officers' shift was routine. Shaquille and Malikul conducted a few traffic stops. A new driver had rolled through a stop sign. A young woman had an expired car registration. Neither of the drivers had outstanding **warrants**. The officers issued only warnings.

Several hours later, the rookies returned to the station. Feeling proud, they knew they had saved a life that day. It was time to write up their incident reports.

Chapter 2

FOLLOWING THE SCENT

Officer Kaitlyn Sawyer strode to the police car with purpose. On her command, Otto jumped in the back, and the pair set off. They had just received an urgent K-9 call.

K-9 is a play on the word *canine*, which means dog. Otto was a large German shepherd. Like many other dog handlers, Kaitlyn cares for her animal round the clock. Otto was playful, even affectionate, at home with her. But when Kaitlyn suited up, he became alert. His ears perked up. Otto was a working dog.

During the short drive, Kaitlyn considered what she might be called on to do. K-9 units help find and arrest fleeing suspects. They recover **evidence** on crime-related calls. But this call was for search and rescue.

At the scene, another police officer filled Kaitlyn in. She listened carefully. A family had reported a missing person to Maine's Kennebunk Police Department.

◀ **Police dogs uncover evidence that officers can't see or smell. K-9 teams also help in search and rescue jobs.**

Kaitlyn and Otto quickly got to work. Otto pulled hard on the police lead. The German shepherd moved swiftly. He worked with a clear focus. Kaitlyn sprinted along behind him, the lead in her hand. She was breathing heavily. This highly trained dog was tracking the smell of a person.

Otto had picked up the freshest scent from the ground. Sometimes it's rubber from a shoe. Other times, it's sweat on a piece of clothing. Once Otto found a knife that a suspect had discarded in a field. This time it was a human scent on some bramble in the woods.

One, two, three uneasy minutes went by. After two more minutes of tracking, the team had located the target in a clearing. The 80-year-old man had wandered away from home. He was suffering from **dementia**. When Kaitlyn and Otto found him, the man was confused but unharmed. They introduced themselves and called it in. Then they brought him back to his family safely.

Police officers sometimes must act as caregivers, parents, or counselors. They should be familiar with mental illness. They must also be informed about drug abuse.

Next up for Otto and Kaitlyn was training for a new certification. They would learn how to locate illegal drugs. It's called **narcotics** detection.

K-9 dogs detect explosives for police ▶ departments and the US military.

BISHOP

SILENCE
=
COMPLICITY
BLACK LIVES MATTER
BLACK LIVES MATTER
JUSTICE
CANNOT
and will not
WAIT
IS VIOLENCE

Chapter 3

GETTING TO A MUCH BETTER PLACE

Stephon Clark died on March 18, 2018. He was in his grandmother's backyard in Sacramento, California. Police officers took his life. They wrongly thought he was armed. Stephon, 22 years old, was Black. Police killings of Black Americans are three times more likely than of whites.

Daniel Hahn joined the Sacramento Police Department when he was 19. Today, he is its first Black police chief. He constantly works toward better policing. "Getting to a much better place" is always on his mind.

Good police officers stay calm and think clearly. They have to make solid judgments under pressure. They must know how to defuse, or de-escalate, conflicts.

◄ **Activists protest recent killings of Black people by police officers. Many police departments are training officers to avoid conflicts and defuse tense situations.**

Sacramento police began a new kind of training in 2019. It uses virtual reality. Police officers wear headsets and wrist sensors. They have virtual weapons. The technology re-creates recent 911 calls. They can even use body camera video.

The training helps officers prepare for high-risk conflicts. It helps them perform under stress. They make decisions about the use of force. They practice speaking out in groups when something isn't right. The training also covers **bias**. That's when someone is unaware of beliefs they hold about others.

Law enforcement and community members across the United States are working to build trust and improve relationships between police officers and citizens. ▶

POLICE

KING
Soopers
HOW MANY
MORE?

Chapter 4

INSIDE THE BOULDER SHOOTING

It was just after 2:30 p.m. on March 22, 2021. The weather was cold and gray in Boulder, Colorado. Snow was still on the ground.

911 calls were coming in all at once. There was a frightening situation at a local grocery store. A gunman had opened fire.

Local police responded immediately. Officer Eric Talley was the first to arrive on the scene. An 11-year veteran of the Boulder Police Department, he was also a father of seven. He entered the building. Inside was the gunman. The officer moved in carefully. His gun was drawn.

As the minutes ticked by, dozens of other police officers flooded the area. Manned fire trucks and ambulances filled the parking lot. Helicopters and **drones** appeared overhead to track what was happening. The teams were in constant radio communication. They shared information about the unfolding crisis.

◀ **People visited this memorial honoring the victims of the Boulder shooting.**

▲ **A SWAT team like this one helped Boulder police officers secure the area and arrest the shooter.**

A nine-person special weapons and tactics (SWAT) team was called in. Armored police vehicles loaded with officers appeared. One had orders to ram through the window of the grocery store.

A hook-and-ladder truck drove next to the building. The crew prepared to lift SWAT team members onto the roof. Its goal was to circle the building and secure all exits.

Police called out on their public address system: "This is the Boulder Police Department. The entire building is surrounded. You need to surrender now!"

By 3:27 p.m., SWAT officers had the suspect in custody. In the cross fire, he had been hit in the leg. It was less than an hour after the first shot had rung out. The crisis was over. The injured suspect was taken to the hospital for treatment, then to the county jail.

At the crime scene, police detectives began to interview witnesses. They collected evidence, took photographs, and recorded notes for their reports. Much work lay ahead to prepare a court case for murder.

Ten people lost their lives that day. Eric Talley was the last fatality. This police officer had put himself in harm's way to protect others.

THINK ABOUT IT

- Which parts of being a police officer appeal to you? Which parts don't appeal to you? Explain your answers.
- Being a police officer requires empathy, which means having understanding and compassion. Give an example of empathy from each police officer story.
- If you were a police chief, how would you work toward better policing?
- What do you think are the biggest challenges to being a good police officer today?

GLOSSARY

bias (BYE-us): A bias is when you have a feeling for or against something without enough reason. It's important for police officers to recognize their own biases.

body camera (BOD-ee KAM-ruh): Police officers often wear body cameras to record activity in front of them. They are sometimes called body cams.

COVID-19 (KOH-vid nine-TEEN): COVID-19 is short for **co**rona**vi**rus **d**isease 20**19**. It is a virus that is easily spread from person to person.

dementia (dih-MEN-shuh): Dementia is a term for the impaired ability to remember, think, and make decisions. Alzheimer's disease is the most common type of dementia.

dispatcher (dis-PATCH-ur): A dispatcher, such as a 911 operator, gets information from the caller and sends out the right kind of help in an emergency.

drones (DROHNZ): Drones are remote-controlled airplanes. Police officers may use a drone to view a scene from a safe distance.

duty belts (DOO-tee BELTS): Police officers wear duty belts to carry some of their equipment and tools, such as a radio.

evidence (EV-ih-duhns): Evidence is facts or signs that help you form an opinion. Police dogs can help recover evidence.

narcotics (nahr-KOT-iks): Narcotics are drugs that are prescribed for pain. They are often addictive.

rookies (RUHK-eez): A rookie is someone in his or her first year of the job. They don't have previous experience.

warrants (WOR-unts): A warrant is an official document. It gives an officer permission to do something. For example, police officers need a warrant to arrest a person.

TO LEARN MORE

Books

Given-Wilson, Rachel. *Your Future as a Police Officer.* New York, NY: Rosen, 2020.

Smith, Elliott. *Use of Force and the Fight Against Police Brutality.* Minneapolis, MN: Lerner, 2021.

Terrell, Brandon. *Police Dogs on the Job.* Mankato, MN: The Child's World, 2017.

Websites

Visit our website for links about police officers: childsworld.com/links

Note to Parents, Teachers, and Librarians: We routinely verify our Web links to make sure they are safe and active sites. So encourage your readers to check them out!

SELECTED BIBLIOGRAPHY

Haynes, Danielle. "Study: Black Americans 3 Times More Likely to Be Killed by Police." *UPI.com.* June 24, 2020. www.upi.com.

Padilla, Ramon, et al. "Closer Look: How the Boulder Shootings Unfolded." *USA Today.* March 24, 2021. www.usatoday.com.

Sullivan, Shawn. "Kennebunk Police Duo Sawyer and Otto Celebrate Sweet Scent of Success." *Seacoastonline.com.* May 29, 2020. www.seacoastonline.com.

Tucker, Emma, Ryan Young, and Julia Jones. "With Virtual Reality Police Training, Sacramento Tries to 'Get to a Much Better Place.'" CNN.com. April 27, 2021. www.cnn.com.

INDEX

ABOUT THE AUTHOR

Emily Dolbear is the author of many books for young readers. She writes and edits from her home in Brookline, Massachusetts.

ADVANCE PRAISE FOR

Innovation and Impact

The Origins and Elements of Ed.D. Program Excellence

"In an era of much conversation about how to improve the Ed.D. in school leadership, the authors throughout this book provides a rare opportunity to look inside innovation within current Ed.D. programs, including initiation and implementation, through to the elements that garner innovation awards for such programs. The Ed.D. programs discussed throughout this volume provide a unique set of perspectives of how to include stakeholders and the community in the innovation process, while also providing a wealth of examples of recovering from mistaken assumptions and directions while building programs that thrive and ultimately serve students and their communities."

Alex J. Bowers, Ph.D., Professor
Teachers College, Columbia University

"I was delighted to preview the book *Innovations and Impact* edited by W. Kyle Ingle and Harriette T. Rasmussen. As the Coordinator of an Ed.D. program that is not a part of the Carnegie Project, I found this book offered incredible insights into what it means to establish an Ed.D. and then improve continuously. The chapters focus on seven award winning programs and a description of their journey was very helpful in rethinking the Ed.D. This book will definitely be a guide as we move forward in refreshing our current Ed.D. and also in pursuing a new Ed.D. in the future. When the book is available, it will have a prominent place on my bookshelf and be used as a guide to support the development of a quality program and scholarly practitioners."

Mary Lynne Derrington, Associate Professor
Ed.D. Coordinator, University of Tennessee, Knoxville

"Some may think the phrase 'innovative doctoral program' is an oxymoron, as the structure and deliverables of this terminal degree have endured for hundreds of years. But, through the work of W. Kyle Ingle and Harriette T. Rasmussen, in *Innovation and Impact: The Origins and Elements of Ed.D. Program Excellence*, that thought is proven false. In a series of chapters that build from the work of Lee Shulman and a set of guidelines that form the backbone of the Carnegie Project on the Education Doctorate organization, the collective wisdom of prize-winning pacesetters is shared. Each contribution, in this amazing compendium, reflects an exceptional program ranging from a private urban university to a collaborative group of five state institutions. By describing these compelling redesigns, readers will be privy to what is sometimes hidden from competitors—the "secret sauce" that makes the program attractive to applicants and produces the most outstanding Ed.D. students. In this compilation there are powerful examples of self-study strategies, ways to center doctoral candidates in the trialing of new programmatic ideas, unique advising models, and frank descriptions of challenges and rethinking even after being declared a winning program. For longstanding programs, newly established Ed.D. degrees, and future award applicants, this resource is a must read!"

Karen S. Karp, Professor
Johns Hopkins University

"This helpful, clearly-written, and timely volume highlights the recent work of winners of the CPED program of the year, offering useful real-world examples of how to design an education doctorate for scholar-practitioners. These programs all focus on the contemporary needs of students rather than existing traditions. The book thus informs other aspiring programs as well as scholars of change and scholars of higher education, as it emphasizes the successes and frustrations of innovating within highly structured and often inflexible university contexts."

Joanne M. Marshall, Ed.D., Professor
Educational Leadership, Organizations, and Policy
School of Education, Iowa State University
US Fulbright Scholar to University of Namibia, 2022

"*Innovation and Impact* is a valuable resource for Ed.D. coordinators and faculty committed to excellence and driving social justice in higher education. Through real accounts of exemplary programs' growth and triumph over significant challenges, this book offers practical insights for improvement and sustainability. This book serves as a compass for navigating Ed.D. program success in today's higher education landscape."

Frank Perrone, Assistant Professor and Ed.D.
Program Coordinator
Educational Leadership
Indiana University-Bloomington